First paperback edition December 2021

Printed by Blurb, Inc. in the United States of America

ISBN 9781736792902 (paperback)
ISBN 9781736792919 (ebook)

Library of Congress Control Number: 2021904866

Published by Lena M. Sakalla
www.lenasakalla.com/books

Many thanks to you and all those who have supported this project along the way. Your love means more than the world to me.

This is for all those curious enough to love.

You are now entering YOU-topia.

9:53AM

What if?

 I hum a duet, featuring mischievous Hope herself
 Name a more perilous game to play

What if?

 No, do not think further.
 Impending danger ahead.
 It's a trap for an idealist
  a romantic
  a free spirit
  who easily floats from the dirt
  i n b e t w e e n
  her toes
  up
  to
  her garden
  in the
  s k y

What if
 you thrive off the high of feelings. . .
What if
 you are also overly venturesome with your resilient heart. . .
What if
 our blazing connection activates your internal fire alarms. . .
What if
 I grabbed your hands and said let's fall in l o v e. . .
What if
 the expiration date is in 24 hours–
 would you say y e s. . .
What if
 we defy the expiration date. . .
What if?

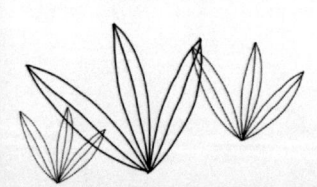

10:41AM

O   P   E   N
unrestricted   exchanges
both ways

Talk to me
               I do.
Talk to me
               You do.

My colorful words twirl and splatter your walls
Your thoughts plant stars on the ceiling
Our discussions are art in the making.

                                                secure

    honest

                    peaceful

         comfortable   excited

                              Here I feel safe.
                                    You
                                  are safe.
                    Our minds waltz in conversation
              as if they had been training closely for years
           This is not because we find unabridged agreeance
                           but because we are seeking
                        a greater awareness of the other
                        Fluently, we alternate who leads
                           without missing a beat.

My thoughts have never felt so liberated in the presence of another.

11:02AM

We should get up.

We should stay in bed.

Your eyes are
deep pools
of dark browns intertwined
with uneven swirls of blonder strands
that frolic within your irises
Your pupils
enlarge with curiosity and
examine my face for answers
analyzing my opinions for understanding
They are eager for new data.
As I gaze back into them
I peer into the workings of your psyche
If I thought your features were gorgeous, your mind
is showstopping.
I wonder if you know
just
how
incredible you are
How exceptional a soul like yours really is
Maybe if you truly grasped your invaluable treasures within
you wouldn't pursue challenges that
threaten its existence
those that potentially damage its striking beauty
So
maybe you don't know. . .
maybe
you can't *see* it. . .

1:39PM

Cue
"I've Got A Crush On You" -
Live At Zardi's, 1956
from 1:11-2:44

Thank you, Ella Fitzgerald
Queen of Jazz.

Close your eyes and listen.
Only continue afterwards.

2:21PM

Water.
     My favorite element.
     Sprinkled droplets daintily decorate
     my body, like how paint
     dresses a canvas.
Soap bubbles
     belong to Head & Shoulders
     instead of a proper bar.
     Boys.
     Suds wash over my body
     cruising through places I usually keep hidden.
Our eyes lock.
     Sharp inhale.
        My spine erects, awakening its vertebrae colleagues.
          Kiss, but different.
Our
       words
          s l o w

The air becomes heavy
       in the most incredible way
I feel a magnetic pull enticing our hips
Our bodies are close
       but our physicality cannot illustrate the glow within
Dreamlike.

Can I wash your hair?

Hands
     melting every inch
     My cells are elated
     Dilating my blood vessels as they swarm to the surface
     they carry red parade floats
     hoping his hands will notice and
     graze them again.

Pushed up against the wall
 Our bodies mold and sculpt anew.
 Animal instincts.
 Hyperdrive.
 No space between
 You're keen on it.
Slippery, you say?
Shut up and kiss me.
Spin
Stop
Rinse
Repeat
Lips meet feverishly, over and over
I've never felt so intensely awake while simultaneously
subdued in a daze of heavenly tranquility
Nostalgia will kiss me teasingly with this moment in the future.

This is my new favorite place.
You are my new favorite invitee.
When can we do this again?

3:11PM

Mmhmm
I've
got
a
      sweet tooth for you.
I'd like you with a side of
      pancakes
      two eggs sunny side up
      blackberries
      and toast on the side
Got it?
Every meal must include you
Breakfast, lunch, and especially dinner
You drive my taste buds absolutely bonkers.
      Food is essential, but I'm craving something else
          I've been handed the menu, but all I want is

                                      you.

No harm in serving dessert first
As long as you still eat
the
main
meal.

4:32PM

Still thinking about 2:21pm. . .

I respect that you are not a
heavy drinker.

But damn
you better like this cup of tea.
She is strong, hot, and sweet.
Slurp too quickly and she'll burn you silly.
Hesitate too long and she'll freeze over.
Last I checked, she's the only one of her kind.
The first and last one in stock.
You won't unearth another identical in uniqueness.

I know you're parched.
So tell me
when are you going to take a sip?

6:48PM

First place
again.
God, Mario Kart is rigged.

Tell me how you are winning at everything.
Trash talk.
You win *again*.
Talking mad trash.
This is lame and upsetting to both Pride and Ego.
I'm not used to losing.
Trash talk becomes

soft
You spoon me to console me for my losses
Laying sideways with you, I play even worse.
But in this moment
I am also winning

You just don't know it yet.

G   O
     O   F   Y

Silly smiles
Obnoxious jokes
My heart glows through my eyes
It's beautiful how badly you want to make others happy
I hope you know how happy you've made me.

8:25PM

*Discover the **beauty of this person.** Of this moment.*
*Discover the beauty of **this person.** Of **this moment.***
*Discover the **beauty** of this person. **Of this moment.***

I want to do this.
Heart, Body, and **Mind,** please let me do this.

I know you are a firecracker
    but I need you to steady your rate.
I know our defense fortress coordinates are already plugged into the GPS
    but I need you to actively relax.
I know you are a trigger away from spiraling with fear
    but I need you to rationalize and ground your thoughts.
I think this one is *good.*

What will it take for you to trust me?
Will you ever?

9:44PM

The frame of adorable, old-man-style glasses
    rests on your scrunched nose
    as your hands
    glide
    over

    the keys
You miss a note or flub a rhythm and your body flinches with rejection
I giggle to myself
The flaws are unrecognizable
I can only tell they exist because of your body language
Don't give away your secrets, love.
Your beautiful music is more than I could fathom learning
It's unexpectedly romantic
In a trance, I cup my hands below my ribs
to catch my heart in case it falls
Cheap yet effective insurance, I'm sure.

Your music is. . .

      This is so. . .

            nice.

If only you were going to be
a physics teacher

11:47PM

When's your next piano recital?
You're the loveliest boy I've ever met.
I love your sweet kisses.
I gush
when your tangled, curly eyelashes
protest a synchronized awakening in the morning.
You're the best cuddler ever.
When you lay in bed with one arm behind your head and you smile
you look like a god.
Goddammit, you better think I'm funny or we're over.
Do you feel our connection?
LIKE ME BACK.
Let's have sex.
Do you actually want to be my friend?

Things I wish I said.

12:52AM

I told you
I'm going to SLEEP
I struggle to reiterate as I fold over laughing
in response to your tickle tactic.
You are ridiculously annoying
       everything I want
       a dose of pure happiness

Then I remember.

We're supposed to be
'just for the weekend', right?
My smile fades and humor fizzles
as the air escaping my body leaves my lips aghast

Oxygen is resurged as you sweep me into a deep, slow kiss
My face cradled in your hands
as your tongue wrestles mine.
Little do you know
my heart is crawling out of my chest
to runaway with yours
They beat in the DJ room next door
Maybe they'll hit it off
Hopefully mine doesn't misbehave
but you know how hearts tend to act. . .

involuntarily.

1:07AM

Roll your
hips into mine
Interlace fingers
Hearts press together
You make me feel
perfect,
but
it scares me more than it reassures me.
Something about this situation flags *caution* in red
I'm at a loss for words, unable to rationalize this sudden
tsunami of anxiety that has crippled my trust
I want my jaw to drop
so the truth can launch off my tongue.
Instead, I close my eyes
and kiss you
hoping my worries will dissipate
Yet, I know this dosage isn't potent enough to cure.

How can I tell you you're perfect
without offsetting our equation?
How do I tell you I want you?
How do I explain when I don't?

This moves quick
Faster
Yes
No.
Too much.
Thoughts hijack my mental stability, poisoning your kisses
Old, haunting memories invade my senses and block you out.
Trauma comes in waves and when it goes untreated
unmapped land mines are conceived
I ignore the burden of truth
so it breeds fragile scars
that fester even when unintentionally provoked.

I see you blame yourself
No, no

My eyes are screaming,
It's me.

Well, could it be him?

No, no.
He is not <u>him</u>.
Breathe in the present
or
you
will
miss
this.
Exhale.

He is not him. He is not him.

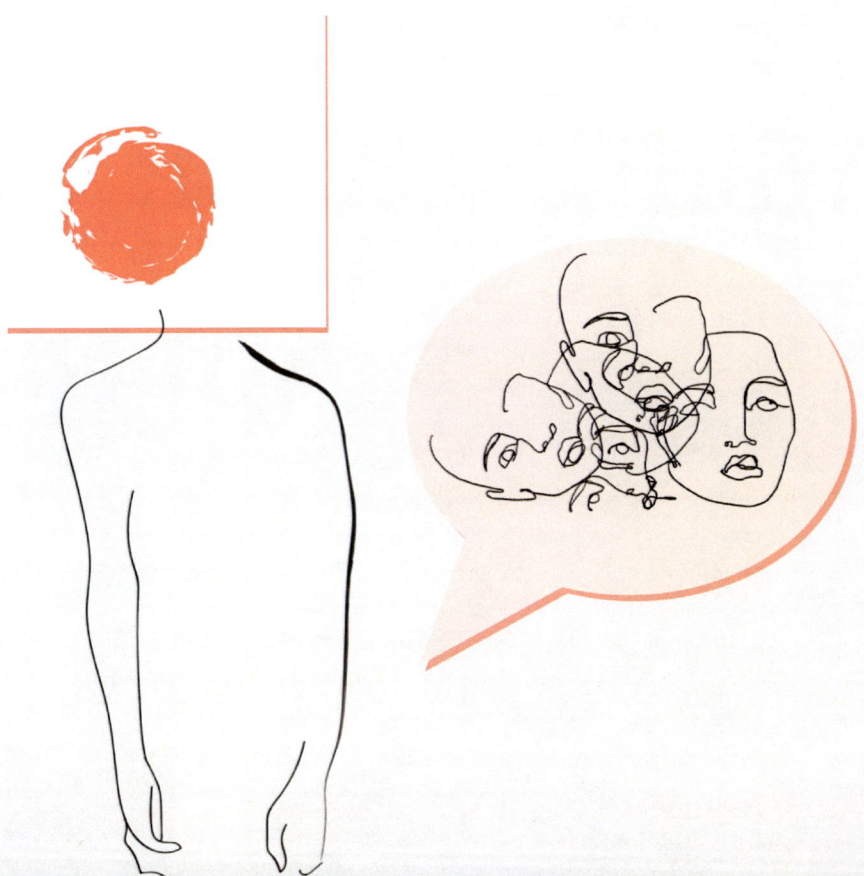

2:34AM

Studying people is a beloved pastime of mine
Unearthing what makes them tick
burst with unimaginable energy
sink
float
But discovering *the switch* is everything
Oh, it's the most astonishing transformation to witness
This is the moment right before one boils to an unbearable temperature
It's proof of our animalistic genetics–
fueled by adrenaline and
sensational lust.

When I found your *switch*,
your changeover was as expected
but the aftermath yielded unforeseen results
unprecedented even
Aggression, speed, and roughness never settled in.
You turned
soft
Your voice and touch
soft
Diabetically sweet and in no tussle with Time.

Dumbfounded
I am
No words
have I
I must have entered

You-topia

How surreal.

3:49AM

. . .Hello, may I speak to Time?
. . .I need to ring in a favor.
. . .How much can I buy?

4:06AM

4:36AM

I guess he's asleep.

>His soft arms have wrapped me into a snuggle
>>The only one I want
>His legs rest, sandwiching mine with
>>our hips diagonally offset
>His heart thumps into my back
>>while mine conducts with the offbeat
>His breathing on my neck is rhythmic, soothing music
>>and makes me smile into the pillow
>Our bodies
>compliment each other and
>compose sweet
>lyrical refrains
>A happy coincident of a duet

I hope his dreams are kind to him.
I guess I'll fall asleep now.

5:54AM

Birds are singing love songs in the trees adjacent to your window.

What I really need them to do is
      shut the hell up
I groan and shift a bit in defiance
You don't like that
so you
         pull

                  me

                      back

                          closer to you.
I sigh
perfectly content with the play.

I'll let him sleep another hour. . .

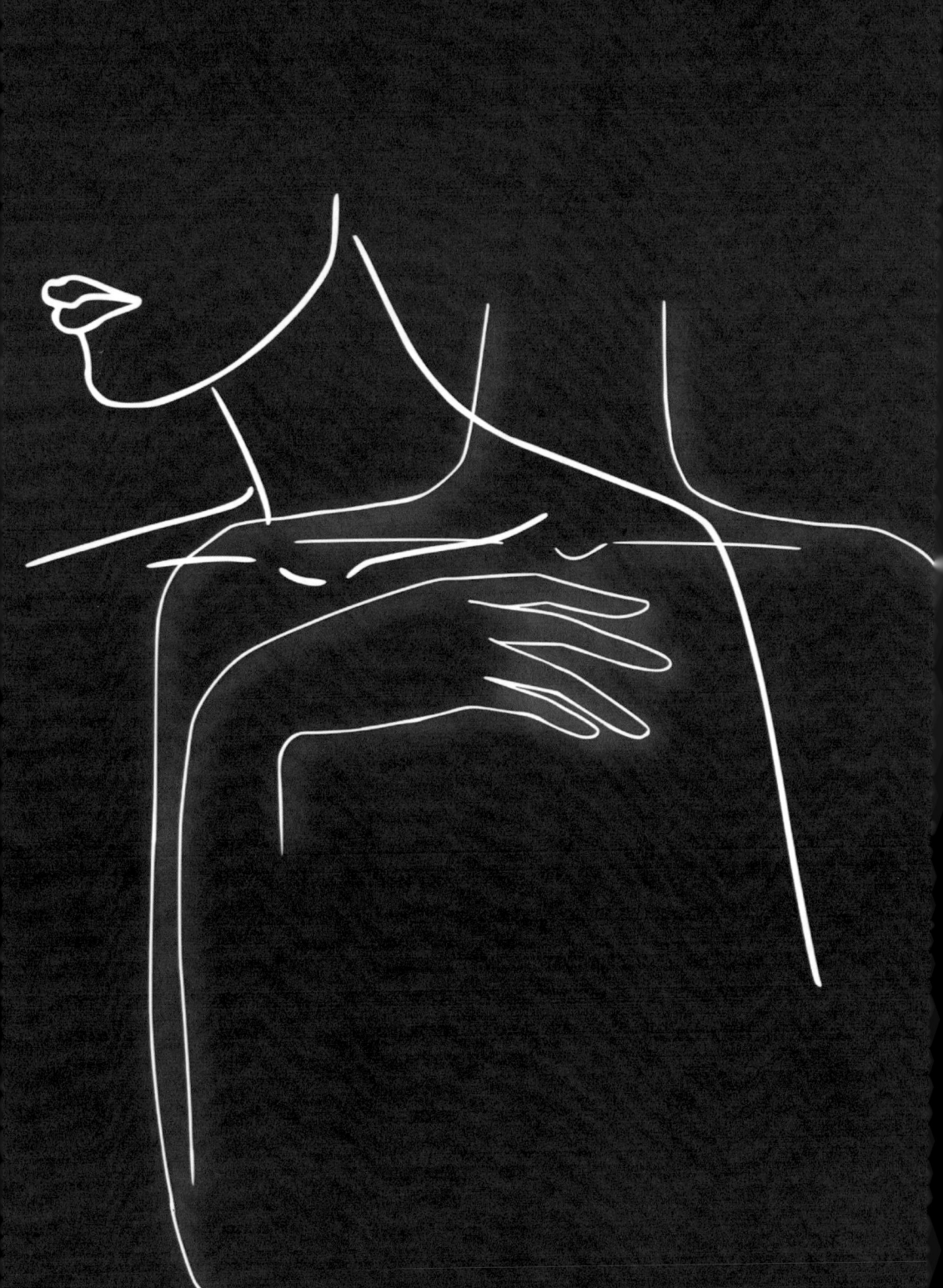

6:17AM

Footsies.
Our toes articulate *'good morning'* before the rest of our bodies can
Can you blame them for wanting in on some of the affection?
Still again.
Breathing.
Soft inhale and exhale
Soundly
Safe
Calm

My head is not getting the memo
the noise inside is chaotic
Mad, even

Heavier inhale and exhale
You did this

My mind is in a frenzy
trying to categorize

You

But it keeps failing to compute
our statement
It has never calculated anything like this
The system is about to combust with
flower scents
gooey feelings
and images of

You

Breathing.
Just inhale and exhale

Wow.
This *is* wild.

7:23AM

Kisses.
Early morning kisses
Quick, soft
k i s s e s s .
Touch dances up and down my curves
Your index finger uses invisible ink to cover me in doodles
Goose bumps bud and populate original ghost towns that
      chase after your stroke.
Rise and fall
Quick, soft
Pitter, patter, my heart hums
Flip, flop, tummy talk
Don't stop.
Even the sun doesn't want to interrupt our intimacy
as it slowly peeks through the blinds, longing for permission to enter
before it seeps down the wall
and tip toes chromatically across the keyboard
Suddenly and without proper notice
it loudly fills the room.
Bright, soft colors of a yolk
Your foolish smile radiates greater warmth
without a doubt
Your stubborn, swollen lips part in compliance
with your pearly teeth so they may also witness our beauty.

The sun is on full volume and
so   are   we
Wrapped in each other–
our limbs are eager to become familiarized with every crevice of the other.
The passion intensifies.

Quick, soft
Kisses.
My eyes drunkenly crack mid-kiss
to see if it's true.

Quick, soft
on my lips
across my cheek
along my jaw
down my neck
between my collar bones.
The sun and your fingers boogie as one around my belly button
You never told me you were a fan of the Blues.
Stunning. Blazing. Breathless.

Quick, soft
Heaven in a bed
God, don't let this be the end.

8:15AM

What are you most afraid of?
Do you see yourself getting married? Or having kids?
What's your favorite song?
  Can I show it to you?
Have you ever been in love?
  What's it like?
Will you sing to me? Please? Play, please?
Why are you perfect at everything you do?

Why did you come here?

This.

This is why I came.

About the author

Lena Sakalla is an actress, tree-hugger enthusiast, and BFA graduate from the University of West Florida. Since 2020, she has spent her time in Spain. When Lena isn't immersed in the arts, she can be spotted frantically studying languages, adventuring in the mountains, or spending time with her loved ones. 24 hours in YOU-topia is her debut poetry book and materialized COVID-19 project, which prompted her reflections on the absurd beauty in life that manifests when following one's gut.

www.ingramcontent.com/pod-product-compliance
Lightning Source LLC
Chambersburg PA
CBRC091533240626
47164CB00007B/171